The Truffle Mouse

Look out for more books by Holly Webb

A Cat Called Penguin
The Chocolate Dog
Looking For Bear
A Tiger Tale

For younger readers:
Magic Molly

For slightly older readers:
The Animal Magic stories

www.holly-webb.com

The Truffle Mouse

HOLLY WEBB

Illustrated by Hannah Whitty

■ SCHOLASTIC

First published in the UK in 2015 by Scholastic Children's Books
An imprint of Scholastic Ltd
Euston House, 24 Eversholt Street
London, NW1 1DB, UK
Registered office: Westfield Road, Southam, Warwickshire, CV47 0RA
SCHOLASTIC and associated logos are trademarks and/
or registered trademarks of Scholastic Inc.

Text copyright © Holly Webb, 2015
Illustration copyright © Hannah Whitty, 2015

The rights of Holly Webb and Hannah Whitty to be identified
as the author and illustrator of this work have been asserted by them.

ISBN 978 1407 14486 3

A CIP catalogue record for this work
is available from the British Library.

Printed and bound by CPI Group (UK) Ltd, Croydon, CR0 4YY
Papers used by Scholastic Children's Books are made
from wood grown in sustainable forests.

1 3 5 7 9 10 8 6 4 2

This is a work of fiction. Names, characters, places, incidents
and dialogues are products of the author's imagination or are used fictitiously.
Any resemblance to actual people, living or
dead, events or locales is entirely coincidental.

www.scholastic.co.uk
www.holly-webb.com

For Madeleine

Alice pulled her boots on slowly, frowning at Dad. "But why are we going out for lunch?" she asked. "We always have Saturday brunch at home. Always." She couldn't understand why the plans had suddenly changed. She'd been looking forward to one of Dad's bacon sandwiches; and now he'd bought a blender, he made banana smoothies too. What did they have to go out for? She didn't feel like going anywhere. All she wanted to do was sit at the kitchen table in her onesie and eat one of Dad's sandwiches.

"We're meeting Tara." Dad was beaming

at her, but he looked worried underneath the smile. As if he wasn't sure Alice was going to be happy about it. Alice looked at him sideways. Tara was Dad's girlfriend – he'd been with her for about six months, and Alice had met her a couple of times. She was all right. Nice-ish.

"Come on, we'll talk about it in the car." Dad shooed her out of the house. He was avoiding telling her something, Alice decided. It was going to be something she didn't want to do.

Once they were on the main road, driving into town, Alice heard Dad take a deep breath. "So! I thought we'd go to that new soft play place and then get lunch."

Alice blinked. "Soft play?"

"Er, yes, Tara's bringing her little girl, you see. Tilly's a bit younger than you."

"I didn't know that. . ." Alice muttered. She could feel Dad trying not to sigh.

"I talked to you about her, Alice."

"Do we have to go to soft play? I don't really feel like it. . ." she said mulishly.

"Oh. . . But Tara's meeting us there, in the coffee shop," Dad murmured. "We're almost late, actually. We don't have to stay very long, if you don't want to. We'll go and have some lunch. Pizza? That would be good, wouldn't it? Here we are, look."

I know. I can see that we're in the car park for the soft play place. I'm not two. . . Alice didn't actually say it. She didn't say anything. She just got out of the car, wishing that Dad would stop smiling and being so cheerful.

"There they are!" Dad sped up, hurrying Alice over to meet Tara. A girl in a purple furry coat was sitting on Tara's lap. She looked about five, Alice reckoned. Around the size of the little ones in reception at school. They looked alike – it was so obvious she didn't need more than that one glance. Dark eyes and dark, wavy, messy hair. Alice immediately resolved to start wearing tidy plaits. She didn't ever want people calling her and Tilly sisters.

Alice hung back, watching Dad hug Tara – the smaller girl ducked her head round behind Tara's shoulder and didn't let him hug her, which just made Dad do his super-happy smile again.

Tara seemed to be even more nervous than Dad. She kept laughing in a silly way and trying to get Tilly to talk to Alice. But neither of them said anything.

"Maybe you two could go and play?" Tara suggested, but she sounded a bit doubtful, and Tilly just turned her face away.

Dad got Alice a hot chocolate, but she didn't drink it. She went and climbed up the scramble net, and up to the very top part of the soft play stuff, where the highest slide started. From there she could see right down into the coffee shop, and she watched Dad and Tara holding hands, and talking. Dad was patting her. As though he was telling her that everything would be OK. Everything with Alice.

Tilly had got off her mum's lap, at last. She

was in the ball pond – she was watching Tara
and Dad, just like Alice was.

Alice leaned out between two padded bars,
staring at them as Tilly raced back through
the tables to Tara and her dad. Dad gave her a
hug, and this time she let him. Tilly was cute.
Little and cute.

Alice swallowed. She was sort of used to Tara being around. Dad had a photo of her on the kitchen windowsill. Alice didn't mind her all that much. Mostly it was still just Dad and Alice on their weekends. Tara didn't change anything – except that she'd made Alice realize that Mum and Dad really weren't going to get back together.

And now there was Tilly. All at once. And everything seemed different.

Alice looked at her dad and Tara from across the table. They were only about a metre away from her, but it felt like there was a gap between her and them a mile wide. They kept glancing at each other and smiling. Alice wasn't actually sure that her dad had remembered she was there.

"Oh! Yes, we need to order," he muttered, grabbing for the menu as the waiter stood over them impatiently. "Mmmm, Alice, what are you going to have?"

"Can I have a pizza with ham on, please?" Alice asked the waiter, very politely. She felt like she had to make up for her dad being clueless. And Tara as well. Because, Alice realized with sudden horror, the waiter probably thought that Tara was her mum. And Tilly was her little sister. Alice gulped her apple juice, spilling it a little because her hand was shaking.

"Don't you want olives on it too?" her dad asked, smiling at her.

Alice blinked at him, confused. Why on

earth would she want olives? She *hated* olives. They tasted weird and salty and horrible, and they looked nasty too, like dead beetles, or something. She had never, ever ordered olives on a pizza.

Her dad went red, very slowly, his cheeks flushing scarlet, and then the colour seeping into his stubbly throat as well. "Um, no, of course not. Er, I'll have pepperoni, please." Tara ordered her pizza, and pasta for Tilly, and the waiter hurried away, leaving Alice and Dad staring at each other.

"Sorry, I forgot you don't like olives," Dad said, trying to smile.

"But you don't like them either." Alice frowned at him. "What made you even think of them? I *never* have them."

Tara was looking worried now too, fiddling with her cutlery as though she was nervous. "I think your dad just got mixed up," she put in, her voice extra friendly and helpful. "Tilly really loves olives. We've brought her here for lunch a few times. That's all."

Tilly glanced up from her drawing and stared at Alice. She looked so sweet, Alice felt like knocking over her glass. Or stealing the crayons.

She swallowed, which was hard, because there was a great lump of something stuck in her throat. She wasn't sure if it was miserableness or fury. "You got me mixed up with Tilly?" she said to Dad.

"Oh well, it wasn't like that," Dad said quickly. "I just got confused for a minute."

But he had. It was obvious. He'd forgotten what Alice liked, because this other girl, this Tilly, was more important.

Alice didn't really eat much of her pizza. It couldn't have tasted worse if it had been covered with olives.

2

"Can we go?" Alice stood next to her mum, with her coat on, eyeing the empty plate. "You said after lunch. You *have* finished."

"Actually, I was thinking of having an apple…" But her mum was only teasing, Alice could tell. "Yes. All right. You've been very patient, actually. Where were you all morning? I thought you'd be hanging around in here begging to have lunch at half-past ten."

Alice handed her a fistful of papers, covered in drawings. "I was doing these," she explained. They were covered in tiny, delicate drawings, in her newest felt tips, the ones Dad had given her the weekend before. "It's a list, do you see?" she explained to her mum. "All the things a hamster needs."

"Really? All of this?" her mum murmured, turning the pages round to peer at the edges – the paper was covered. "I thought a hamster just needed a cage. And food. Alice, this isn't a cage!" She pointed to a lacy-looking pink and purple building. "It's a hamster *palace*! There's a flag on top of it!"

"I know." Alice leaned over it admiringly. "It would be so cool to have a hamster cage with towers... There's an under-the-sea one on the other side. And that's a space hamster ship." She patted her mum's shoulder. "It's all right, Mum, I know there won't be a hamster palace at the pet shop. I was just getting excited, that's all. I've been looking forward to this weekend so much. The week was so long, it felt like it was going on for ever. Especially school." She made a face. "I know it'll just be a cage. Although, actually, when I looked online, one of the pet websites had a cage that did look sort of spaceship-like – all coloured tubes for the hamster to climb through – it's really cool. Lucy's hamster has a cage a bit like that too, just not as many bits sticking out." Lucy was Alice's best friend from school; she'd been given a hamster for her birthday, a couple of months before. Alice riffled to the back of the stack of papers and showed her mum a page she'd printed.

Her mum frowned a little, turning the paper sideways. "It does look very smart. Does it, ummm, does it keep them in?"

Alice blinked at her, not sure what she meant.

"I mean, the hamster can't get out?" her mum asked worriedly. "All those tubes. It looks a bit fragile. The hamster wouldn't be able to escape?"

Alice leaned against her shoulder. "How can you be scared of a hamster?" she giggled. "They're *tiny*."

Her mum sighed. "I'm not really scared, I just don't want to go into your bedroom and find a hamster asleep in your washing basket, or something like that. I've never had a little pet, you know that. Only cats. I'm sure I'll love a hamster once I get used to it, though," she added quickly.

*

Alice wasn't sure her mum would get used to a hamster. She was trying to cheer up Alice by buying her one. It was because Ms Hickman, Alice's teacher, had told Mum and Dad at Parents' Evening earlier on that week that Alice "sometimes seemed a little sad" and "was very quiet this week". Alice knew exactly what she'd said because she'd been waiting outside in the hallway at school and Mum and Dad had discussed it in hissing whispers all the way back to their cars. They hadn't thought Alice was listening, but of course she was.

Alice didn't realize she was any quieter than usual. It was odd. She supposed Ms Hickman would notice, though. It made her wonder what her teachers had said about her before.

Mum always just came home from Parents'
Evening and said that it was fine, but she
needed to be neater with her handwriting, or
something like that.

Mum and Dad would never have let her
hear them saying that kind of thing before,
but they were so cross with each other that it
seemed as though they'd forgotten Alice was
there. Which was funny when it was her they
were talking about. She'd felt like joining in,
and saying of course she was sad. What did
they expect? They'd sold her lovely house,
the house she'd always lived in, with her own
proper bedroom. And now she had to get used
to two new not-so-nice houses, and nothing
was ever in the right place when she wanted it.
And now there was Tilly. Her dad was going

to be somebody else's dad too. Wasn't she allowed to be sad? Weren't *they* sad about what had happened?

Alice wasn't sure. Maybe Dad wasn't sad at all.

Alice gathered up her drawings of hamster cages carefully and gave her mum a quick one-armed hug. She didn't understand how anybody could not want a hamster in their house – they were so soft! And the little black eyes, like beads! But she knew that Mum didn't, really didn't. She was only doing it to make Alice happy.

"I can't believe we're going to the pet shop today," she murmured. "I've wanted a hamster for so long."

"Last week you said we ought to get a Shetland Pony," her mum pointed out.

Alice hugged her tighter. "I know. I didn't really mean it, though. You made a face when I was talking about what colour hamster I'd like to get. So I thought I'd better make you grateful I was starting with a small animal."

"Very clever." Her mum snorted. "Cunning. And don't think that starting off small with a hamster means I'll let you get something else bigger in a few months. A hamster. One hamster. That's it. Poor Tiger's already going to think you don't love him any more."

Alice did love Tiger, of course she did. But he was Mum's cat – he adored Mum, and he always wanted to sit on her lap. He only sat on Alice if she'd got to her mum's lap first, and then she was just a sort of cushion that had got in the way... Tiger didn't mind if Alice picked him up, but he'd only keep still for about ten seconds, then he would wriggle firmly away. A hamster would be *hers*.

Alice smiled sweetly. "Yes, Mum." She hauled her mum up out of the chair, and whisked her plate over to the sink. Then she scooped up her mum's handbag and the car keys, pressing them into her arms.

"I might need the loo..." her mum muttered.

Alice glared at her. "If I did that, you'd say I was being *deliberately difficult*. Please let's go!"

Her mum planted a kiss on the top of Alice's tangled brown hair – she'd been running her fingers through it while she was drawing.

"I'm ready really. Come on. It'll only take ten minutes to get there."

Alice gave her a sudden, panicked look. "What if they don't have any hamsters?" she asked, frozen in the middle of the kitchen. "I didn't think of that."

"They do, I phoned them the other day to check," her mum said calmly. "They said they always have several and not to worry."

"Oh. . ." Alice breathed in shakily. "OK. Thanks, Mum. I'm just so excited. It would be awful if we couldn't get a hamster today."

"Alice, it wouldn't be the end of the world." Her mum eyed her worriedly. "You do know the hamster might not be all that friendly to start with, don't you? You won't be upset if it doesn't want to be cuddled?"

"No." Alice followed her out to the car. "I won't, I promise." She thought about it for the whole drive, though. What if the hamster just didn't like her? Sometimes people just didn't like each other. There were a couple of people at school who didn't like *her*, even though she'd never even looked at them the wrong way. What if she never made friends with it? That would be almost worse than no hamster at all. . .

The pet shop cheered her up though – it was lovely. Alice had been there a couple of times before when she'd persuaded Dad to let her go in and look when they were on the way to the hardware shop down the road. The man in the shop didn't mind if you didn't actually buy anything. Alice guessed he was used to people coming in to coo over the hamsters and the guinea pigs. Last time there had been a gorgeous grey rabbit, with soft, floppy ears. But Mum had said no to rabbits when she'd asked before. Too much work, and their new garden was mostly patio. Alice had bought a book on hamsters instead, and told the man that one of these days she was coming back to buy the real thing.

He smiled at her from behind the counter as she peered round the door. "The hamster girl!"

Alice beamed at him. "I'm actually allowed to buy one today," she told him, grinning. "And the cage, and everything."

"You know where they are." He waved her towards the back of the shop, which was covered in a wall of cages. "There's a lovely cinnamon girl and a cream long-haired. Lot of work grooming him, though – you might not want to be doing that with your first hamster."

"Long-haired?" Mum stared down the aisle towards the cages. "I thought – well, I thought a hamster was a hamster, to be honest. . ."

The pet shop man grinned at her. "Syrian, Dwarf, Russian, Roborovski . . . short-haired, long-haired, Rex and Satin." He shook his head at Alice's mum, who was gazing at him in horror. "Don't worry, I'm only teasing you. All ours are short-haired apart from that cream male. And I wouldn't recommend the smaller breeds for you – too wriggly and fast. You want a nice, cuddly Syrian for a first pet."

"Yes..." Alice's mum agreed, a little doubtfully.

Alice caught her hand and pulled her down the aisle to look in the cages. Most of the hamsters were dozing in the little bedrooms, half hidden by piles of litter, or fluffy bedding. "Oh, they're all plump and snuggly!" Alice whispered. "Look at the lovely reddish one! And this one's got spots!"

"Cute," her mum agreed. "He looks like a tortoiseshell cat. He's really unusual, isn't he? I didn't know hamsters came in all those colours."

"Or a little bear." Alice pressed closer to the cage, watching the grey and peach hamster lumber determinedly through the woody stuff on the floor to his food bowl. "He's so funny!"

"So, would you like him?" Alice's mum was trying to sound cheerful and enthusiastic. "I'll go and look at the cages."

"Maybe," Alice murmured back. "Have we seen all of them?" She peered into the cage at the end of the row. "Is there another hamster in here? Oh, look, he's chocolate-coloured, Mum! I can see a bit of his fur under the bedding." She looked round to point the hamster out to her mum, but she'd moved up the aisle to look at all the stuff that they'd need.

The cotton wool bedding shifted a little, as if the creature underneath had heard her notice him. A pinkish-brown nose edged out from under the pile, fringed with delicate silvery whiskers. Alice caught just a glimpse of a shining dark eye. The hamster was watching her. The others hadn't seemed to notice that she and her mum were there – or, at least, they hadn't been all that interested. This one was eyeing her curiously – Alice only wished she could see him too. Or her. She couldn't tell from just a nose and an eye – her hamster book had said that actually it was quite tricky to see the difference, however carefully you looked.

"Come on out and see me," she whispered to the dark-eyed face. "Maybe you're one of those small hamsters that the man was talking about – you don't look quite the same as those big ones. Not from the bits of you I can see, anyway." The little nose twitched and then came out a little further, and Alice smiled.

She wished the man from the shop hadn't said dwarf hamsters were too wriggly. This one was so sweet. Perhaps she could convince the man that she'd be careful?

And then the little dark face came right out from underneath the bedding and stared at her, and Alice stared back.

Not a hamster at all – a tiny, chocolate-brown ball of a mouse.

3

The mouse twitched its whiskers at Alice, and Alice felt herself smile – he was so lovely. So pretty and delicate and curious-looking. The hamsters were gorgeous, but somehow the chocolate mouse made her want to laugh.

"Did you decide?" Mum came back down the aisle, with the man from the shop – Pete, it said on his badge – following her. "Are we having the spotty one? There are some lovely cages – even one with turrets, like your hamster palace."

Alice caught her arm. "Mum, look! Isn't he beautiful?"

"Oh, Alice… That's not a hamster…" Her

mum's voice was horrified.

Alice glanced up at her in surprise. "I know. It's a mouse," she said, frowning. "Mum, please could I have a mouse instead? This one's so lovely. Look, his fur's all chocolatey. Like cocoa powder!"

"I don't think a mouse is a good idea." Mum shook her head decisively. "They're just not—" Alice could tell she was searching for the right words. "They're just not nice. I mean, they're a pest, aren't they? People get rid of mice! Tiger hunts them!"

Alice put her hand up to the cage – she did it without thinking, as though she could cover the poor mouse's paper-thin ears. Mum would be talking about traps next! The mouse stepped cautiously across the cage, as though he'd like to sniff her fingers. Alice's mum shuddered as she saw his pinkish tail.

"Fancy mice are quite different to house mice," Pete put in gently. "They're bred to be friendly, and they don't carry any diseases or anything like that. They're just as clean as hamsters, I promise you."

"But it's so little – like those little hamsters you said weren't a good idea!"

"Mice are actually easier to tame than hamsters. They're very friendly, and if you handle them a lot, they're very calm and gentle. Honestly, even though you think of them darting about really fast, they can be so relaxed." He smiled. "I'm a mouse fan, can you tell? We just don't tend to stock many mice; hamsters are more popular."

Alice's mother nodded, as though she could understand why. She was looking regretfully at the hamsters, as though she had changed her mind about not being keen on them now.

"This is a little male, about eight weeks old – we've sold the rest of his litter already."

Alice smiled at the mouse, who had his tiny pink hands up against the glass side of his tank now. She splayed her own fingers out against the other side of the glass, and he dabbed his nose at them. "He's so handsome," she murmured. "I love his colour. I know we came for a hamster, but couldn't I have a mouse instead, Mum, *please*? Imagine a little tame mouse!"

"But the tail. . ." her mum whispered. "I just can't like mice, Alice. I won't be able to help clean him out, or anything."

"I don't mind! I'll do it all by myself!"

"Every five days or so," Pete told her. "Boy mice can be a bit smelly if you don't make sure to clean the cage out well."

Alice looked sideways at him, raising her eyebrows and shaking her head a little. Couldn't he see that her mum was already trying to find reasons not to have a mouse?

"Sorry. . ." he whispered to her.

"You wouldn't like a hamster after all?" Alice's mum asked, in a persuasive sort of voice.

"Um." Alice looked at the hamsters. The pretty reddish one was flaked out asleep now, she was on her back with her paws in the air, and she was incredibly sweet. But then Alice looked back at the little chocolate mouse, and he was watching her, with his head on one side. His eyes really were like beads, round and sticking out and glittery.

"Would you really hate having a mouse?" Alice asked her mum sadly. She watched her mum look between the two cages and swallow nervously, and she knew that her mum was going to say she couldn't bear a mouse in the house. Alice sighed. She knew what Mum would say. *Ten minutes ago, you were desperate for a hamster...*

"You really, really want this one?" her mum murmured. "I suppose I'll get used to it," she went on slowly, folding her arms tightly across her chest, as though she thought someone might make her stroke a mouse.

Alice blinked – it was so much not what

she'd expected her mum to say that it took a minute to really hear she'd said it. "You mean – yes? We can have one?"

"Yes." Her mum spoke through gritted teeth. "Do they have cages like hamsters?" she asked Pete.

"They can," he agreed. "But mice kick their litter around and it falls out between the wire bars, and they can get their paws caught in cage bars too. You're actually better off with a tank like he's in now. This is a good one." He lifted down a plastic cage to show them.

"That looks like some sort of toy box," Alice's mum said doubtfully. Alice could see what she meant – it was the kind of thing that they'd kept all Alice's Sylvanians in. A deep plastic tray, with a clear lid with wire bars set into it. But inside was an exercise wheel, and all sorts of ramps and shelves. It looked fun.

"It's designed so mice and hamsters can't chew their way out," Pete explained. "No bits to get hold of with their teeth, you see? It's clever."

Alice's mum nodded. She wrapped her arms even tighter around her middle. The thought of escaped mice was making her shiver, Alice could tell.

"It'll be all right, Mum," she whispered. "I could put it on my window seat." That way she'd even be able to see it from her bed. She spun round and caught Pete's sleeve, beaming at him. "What do we take a mouse home in?"

*

Alice sat cross-legged in front of her window seat, watching the little mouse explore his new cage. His tank in the pet shop had been nice – with a little bedroom and a wheel to run on – but she supposed this one must feel like a palace. She had stored his bag of food, the spare bedding and his small travel carry box on the window seat next to the cage. It all looked so smart, and

so organized. It felt important that everything was organized. Not just to show Mum that she really could look after the mouse properly – it made Alice feel better somehow, to have something she knew all about. The little mouse was really hers, and she was going to look after him so well. It was all so *tidy*. And perfect.

"Do you like it?" she whispered to the mouse. "I know you've had a strange day, moving around. And you probably miss the shop. I know how you feel. It's strange, isn't it, being in a new place." She blinked to herself and shook her head, trying not to think about her old house. She still missed it, even after nearly two years. "But I promise I'll look after you." The mouse stopped running determinedly on his wheel and looked over at her, attracted by her voice. He stared at her for a minute and then started to wash his face, licking at his paws and then rubbing them over his fur, just like Tiger did. Alice laughed – she had never realized mice did that too. The mouse's back was arched as he rubbed his nose and ears, and it made him look like a little chocolatey ball.

"You're a truffle," Alice whispered. Truffles were her mum's favourite treat. Alice's dad always used to buy her a box as a present for her birthday. Her mum's favourite kind were little round balls of chocolate cream, covered in cocoa powder, just the colour of Alice's mouse.

"Truffle," Alice called gently, and the mouse looked at her again, and then went back to sleeking his cocoa fur with little pink fingers.

*

Alice spent the rest of the weekend trying to convince Truffle to like her. Mum had got her a book on mice in the pet shop too, and she read the whole thing – although she skipped a lot of the chapter on diseases because it made her feel too scared. She'd read it if Truffle started to look ill.

The book had a long list of things that you could give your mouse for a treat, and Alice wanted to get all of them. Truffle was so tiny, though, he'd probably be full after half a grape. But the book said toast crusts were good, if there wasn't too much butter on them. So on Sunday morning, Alice carefully nibbled away the butteriest bits of her toast and saved him the dry edges.

She put the biggest piece on top of his food bowl, but she held the last little corner in the palm of her hand. Alice sat next to the cage with her hand resting on one of the plastic floors, closer to where Truffle was curled up in the little felt pod that she had chosen for his bedroom. Truffle emerged from his bed and gazed at her. Did he look worried? Alice supposed that suddenly finding a huge hand in his cage was a bit weird. He fiddled with his whiskers, combing at them with his paws, and Alice's eyes widened. She did that! When she was nervous, she fiddled with her hair. Mum was always telling her off about it.

After a few seconds of anxious grooming, though, he sniffed the toast. He stepped slowly towards her, his whiskers twitching with eagerness. Alice bit her bottom lip, trying not to laugh as the gossamer-fine whiskers ran tickling over her fingers. Then he darted the last step forward, seized the piece of toast, and scurried back to eat it. Not all the way back to his bed, but in his exercise wheel. He crouched there, holding the toast in both paws and nibbling blissfully.

On Monday, he had pizza crusts and apple. On Tuesday, a pea pod from the peas her gran had grown in the garden and brought over for Mum. Alice left them in the pod, and Truffle stripped off the outer skin in a couple of quick bites, munching his way in to the jewel-bright peas.

On Wednesday, Alice gave him a dog biscuit – she'd phoned Gran to ask if her dog, Chester, could spare any, and Gran had brought her one over with the peas. It was a bone-shaped biscuit, and it was almost as big as Truffle. He was so excited about the bone biscuit that he climbed on to her hand and hugged it. He had to rest the bottom of it on her palm and stretch his neck up to nibble at the top. It was the first time he'd sat on her – he was so light, she could hardly feel him. The dog biscuit was definitely heavier than he was. He still managed to haul it away with him, though, and he hid it in his bedroom. Then he climbed into the pod and fell asleep on top of it, on guard.

4

By Friday, Alice couldn't understand why she'd
ever wanted a hamster. She nearly drove Lucy
mad at school, going on about how much
fun mice were as pets, and how friendly, and
how tame. It didn't help that Smartie, Lucy's
hamster, had bitten her quite hard on the
thumb when Lucy was only trying to pick her
up for a cuddle.

"Truffle *never* bites," Alice told her smugly.

Lucy rolled her eyes a little, but then she
sighed. "He does sound so cute. Can I come
and see him soon?"

"You could come round after school," Alice

started to say eagerly – but then she sighed. "Oh no, not tonight, it's Friday. I'm going to Dad's for the weekend." She twisted her hair around one finger. She was going to Dad's and poor Truffle would be all on his own. Would he notice? Would he wonder where she was? Usually she looked forward to her weekends with her dad – she missed him, even though he phoned almost every day. But to go to Dad's she had to leave Truffle behind.

Alice hadn't really thought about leaving Truffle until the night before when she'd been packing her rucksack with her pyjamas and some jeans and tops. She always took her things to school and left them in the cloakroom at the back of her class. *Truffle!*

She could hardly pack him in her bag. . . Alice had lugged her bag downstairs to leave it in the hall and gone to find her mum, who was doing some marking for school.

"What am I going to do about Truffle while I'm at Dad's?" she asked anxiously.

Mum looked up at her vaguely. "It's only a couple of days. You'll be back on Sunday night. I'm sure he'll be all right."

"But he needs feeding!" Alice squeaked, staring at her mum in horror. "I can't just leave him! But I don't know what I can do about school. Do you think Dad would let me come home and pick him up?"

Her mother's face seemed to set, her lips thinning into a line. "No," she said, quite flatly. "No, I don't think so. I'm not changing the arrangements now."

Alice wanted to argue, but that face, when they were talking about Dad, meant that it wasn't a good idea. Her parents didn't have screaming rows, and they didn't throw things, or cut photographs in half so nobody could see the other one. They were almost always very polite. But they were angry with each other, still, even two years after they'd split up.

Sometimes Alice felt angry with both of them. But she still knew that it was no use arguing with her mum.

"You'll have to feed him then," she pointed out, hoping that this would change her mum's mind. "I've cleaned out his cage, so you won't need to do that."

Her mother actually put down her pen this time. "Can't you just fill up his food bowl a bit more? He'd be fine."

"*No*, Mum!" Alice shook her head anxiously, and went to stand right in front of her mum – she needed to make her listen properly. "You have to give him nice fresh stuff. Like grapes. And take out anything he's left from the day before in case it goes smelly. I gave him broccoli this morning, but I don't think he liked it, he sort of sniffed it and kicked it away from his bowl." She sniggered. Mice didn't have to have table manners. They didn't always have to "just try a little bit in case you like it". There was no point in her trying a little bit of broccoli, when she already knew quite well it was horrible. She'd been quite pleased that Truffle didn't like it either.

Her mother looked at her silently for a moment, and then nodded. She hugged Alice up against her, pulling her half on to the chair. "All right."

"You'll do it? Would you like me to write you some instructions?" Alice wriggled round to stare at her closely.

"I can just about manage to drop a grape into his cage, I should think. . ." Then her mother's mouth twisted. "I promise I'll look after him for you, but he won't jump out?" she asked anxiously. "Will he— Will he climb on me?"

"I don't think so." Alice eyed her, wondering for about the fiftieth time how she could like mice so much, when she had a mother who was so unbelievably anti-mouse. "You won't smell the same as me. Just make sure you don't leave my door open. You won't, will you? I don't want Tiger to sniff Truffle and go in. Promise you'll be careful."

Alice's room at Dad's house was oddly quiet. It took her ages to get to sleep. She lay there in the almost-dark, watching the slit of light down the side of the door, and trying to work out what was different.

It was as she heard her dad coming upstairs to go to bed that she realized. There was no friendly scrabbling from the mouse cage. No faint squeak from Truffle's wheel, or happy crunching. Her mouse book had explained that mice were nocturnal, even though they were quite happy to be awake during the day too. Truffle adored his wheel, and the wheezing squeak was what Alice drifted off to sleep to now. Her room was too quiet.

"I hope Mum took that apple out of your cage," Alice whispered to an imaginary Truffle. "Do you miss me? I wish she liked you; she could have given you a cuddle..." She rolled over, curling herself into a little ball like a mouse. "Even if you don't miss me yet, I miss you..."

Alice chewed the end of her pencil and sighed. This homework seemed to be taking for ever.

She didn't understand symmetry. She felt as though she ought to, because it was a bit like art and she loved drawing, but she kept getting the answers wrong. Things didn't match up the way she thought they would. Ms Hickman had said that if they got stuck with the homework, they should cut out paper shapes and try turning them round. She said that sometimes it was easier with something real, rather than just trying to see the shapes turning in your head. Gloomily, Alice ferreted in her pencil case for her scissors and started to cut the patterns out of her squared paper. She looked sideways at Dad and Tara, chatting to each other as they chopped vegetables. Tilly was at her grandma's, Tara had explained, when she'd arrived that afternoon.

Dad and Tara were cooking dinner together. She knew where everything was in the kitchen – even some pans that Alice thought were new. Were they hers? Did she cook in Dad's kitchen so often that she'd brought her own pans?

Thinking about it, there was a new chair in the living room too. And other odd things scattered round the house that Alice didn't remember from before.

Alice snapped the scissors together, and her paper shape fluttered to the table in two pieces. She hissed frustratedly and gazed down at it, hot-eyed. Dad didn't even notice. He hadn't asked her about her homework or offered to help like he usually did.

Alice rubbed at her eyes and sighed. She

wasn't going to get this right. Probably she should wait and ask Mum to help tomorrow. She could get out her literacy book instead and do that. But she didn't. Picking up the scissors again, she snipped off the irritating feathery end of hair that kept tickling her chin. If Dad wasn't going to pay any attention to her when she was meant to be doing her homework, she wouldn't do it. The ends spilled across her maths book in a pattern, and Alice smiled to herself. She cut off a bit more. Then she glanced across at Dad and Tara, waiting for them to notice and tell her to stop.

But they were arguing contentedly about the right herbs to put in the pasta sauce, and they didn't notice the wisps of hair trailing over her book. Alice scowled and chopped off another hank, which fell on to her book with a little whispering thump, the hair fanning over the paper.

Then she stopped. Dad wasn't going to notice. Not even if she cut it all off, probably. And if Tara noticed, she'd just smile and smile and say it looked nice. Inside she'd probably think how much nicer her darling Tilly-who-loved-olives was than this stupid girl who cut off her own hair. . .

Alice put her scissors away, her hands shaking, and folded up the hair inside her book.

"Finished?" Dad asked her brightly. "Great timing! Dinner's nearly ready. And Tara and I want to have a chat with you about something."

*

"Where are you going?" Mum spun round to watch Alice sprinting up the stairs. She waved politely at Alice's dad, as he turned away from the gate, and followed Alice up to her room.

"Not even a hug?" she said lightly. "I missed you."

"Mum, he hasn't got any food!" Alice glared at her indignantly. "And there's a bit of mucky apple going disgusting under his wheel."

"I did feed him! Last night."

"Didn't you check his bowl this morning?" Alice demanded. "That apple could have made him ill! Maybe he is ill. . ." she added, looking anxious. "He's all huddled up in his bed. He might be sick."

"He's just asleep, Alice. I'm sorry about the

apple. It can't have been there that long. . ." Then the tone of her voice changed. "Alice, look at me a minute."

Alice concentrated on getting every last tiny scrap of apple out of the cage, and didn't turn round. She should have known it would only take Mum seconds.

"Alice!"

She shut the cage carefully and glanced round at her mum, trying to look innocent. "What?"

"What have you done to your hair?" her mother wailed. "There's a great clump missing!"

"It was an accident," Alice muttered. "I was doing my maths homework, and I— I caught my hair in the scissors, that's all. It doesn't look that bad."

"It looks awful and you've got such lovely hair!"

Alice sat down on her bed and started to cry.

"Oh, Alice love. I didn't mean to say that. You can clip it back, or something." Her mum sat down next to her. "What's wrong? Why on earth did you cut it?"

Alice said nothing. How could she tell her mum that Dad's new girlfriend was moving in with him – and she'd be bringing her little girl? And that now Dad liked Tilly better than he liked her?

5

"Alice! Alice! Have you brought your washing down?" Alice could hear her mum running up the stairs. She hadn't even picked up her washing from the floor. . . Hastily, she grabbed her school blouse and her socks and shoved them in the washing basket. Truffle watched her curiously, sitting on top of the staircase of books she'd made for him to play on.

Her mum opened the bedroom door. "Alice, I said straight after breakfast – tidy up your room and bring your washing down! This room is a tip! Oh, Alice! You've got him out of the cage! Put him back now! Now!"

"Mum, can you shut the door?" Alice watched her mum picking up her feet, as though she was doing some strange dance step. If there'd been a chair to jump on to, she'd probably have leaped on it.

"It's OK. . ." she tried to explain. "He's out, but he's not running around on the floor. He's in his maze, look, I've just finished making it. I just don't want him to see the door open and run out on to the landing, it might be scary for him out there. Or Tiger might come in." Tiger definitely knew that there was something interesting in Alice's bedroom. Several times she had found him sitting outside her door, sniffing curiously.

"Alice, *please*, put the mouse back in the cage," Mum said nervously.

"But it's what it says to do in the book," Alice tried to explain. "You're supposed to give them lots of chances to exercise. And he had to stay in his cage all last weekend, when I was at Dad's. He needs something extra fun. It's going to help me tame him too. I hold the rewards in my hand, look, and he comes towards me through the maze. Oh, he's hiding in the cocoa tin now... It's all right, Truffle... Come on..."

Alice's mum stepped back quickly as the little mouse crept through the cocoa tin – Alice had cut the bottom out so it was a fat tube – and down the plastic bottle that was the next part of the maze. If her mum hadn't been too worried about the mouse inside it, she'd have been impressed. The maze was

like a massive junk model playground; as if a whole nursery class had been let loose on a recycling bin and an unlimited supply of sellotape.

The main part of the maze was a plastic tub that had been full of chocolates, which someone had given to her mum as a thank you present at school. Alice had stuck the ends of plastic bottles and tubes through holes she had made in the sides of the tub, and Truffle was busily scurrying through them all to find the treats that she had hidden. It was clever – but it was also a little fragile-looking, as though it would be quite easy for a determined mouse to escape from.

Alice had started making it as soon as she got home from Dad's the night before. She'd wanted something to do, to be busy with. So she wouldn't have to think about what Dad had told her. And she'd be upstairs, away from Mum, so they couldn't talk about what was wrong and why she'd cut her hair. . .

Alice's mum shuddered as Truffle's pinkish tail whisked through the nearest bottle, and then as he shot out into Alice's cupped hands and started nibbling at the peanuts she was holding.

"See? He's so much tamer already," Alice told her, in between cooing noises. "He's so good! He gets through it really fast, I've been timing him. And if I always give him a treat when he comes to me, I bet I could actually let him run all round my room, and he'll come when I call him."

"I really don't think that's a very good idea—"

"Mum, watch out!" Alice screamed, as she spotted Tiger slinking nosily round Mum's feet. "The cat! Tiger, no!" She flung herself across the room and shut Truffle safely in his cage. Mum tried to catch Tiger, but she tripped over him, and in seconds he was up on the window seat staring hungrily into the cage.

"I told you not to let him out of the cage!" Mum grabbed Tiger and hurried back towards the door, away from Truffle's cage.

"I have to! He's really tame now, but he won't be if I don't handle him! How can I handle him if I never take him out of the cage? And it was you that let Tiger in; why couldn't you shut the door like I told you to?" Alice gasped for breath, and eyed her mum anxiously. She never yelled at her like that. Was she about to lose her pocket money for ever?

Her mum swallowed and closed her eyes, and then sighed as Tiger nudged her cheek lovingly. He was so much her mum's cat; he adored her. "All right. Yes. I'm sorry, I should have checked it was shut properly."

Alice gaped at her. She was right?

"Maybe I could put a sign on my door before I let Truffle out?" she suggested. Her mum's shoulders were hunched over and her eyes looked tired. Alice felt guilty.

"*Free Range Mouse?*" Her mum laughed. "Good idea."

Alice smiled at her – but as her mum turned to go, scooping up the washing basket on her way, Tiger was peering over her shoulder at the mouse cage. Alice didn't think a sign was going to stop him.

She glanced sideways, watching as her mum backed out of the room slowly and shut the door.

6

Alice sat on the wall of the playground next to Lucy, half-listening to her going on and on about her favourite band, and how she really wanted a new pencil case with them on, and her mum was being mean and saying she already had a perfectly good pencil case. Alice nodded sympathetically as Lucy moaned about her dad saying the same thing – he never disagreed with her mum, about anything, ever. . .

Alice flinched a little, but Lucy didn't notice, she just went on and on about how unfair it was. Alice nodded and made tutting noises in the right places, but mostly she was remembering the phone call she'd had with her dad early that morning. Usually, he rang in the evening – he rang most nights. But the night before he hadn't, and he'd explained that he was sorry, he'd been helping Tara and Tilly move into his house. They'd all been a bit tired so he hadn't got round to ringing. He'd thought he'd catch her before school instead.

Alice had gripped the phone tightly, not saying anything. He'd told her that last weekend when she'd been at his house that Tara and Tilly were moving in. But it all seemed to be happening so fast.

"Sorry, sweetheart. You didn't mind that much, me not ringing, did you?"

"No," she whispered.

"Tilly's not sharing your room, you know. She's got the little one by the bathroom."

"OK."

That was about all she'd said for the whole conversation. Her dad had tried, but in the end he'd lapsed into silence too, and then he'd told her to have a good day, and he'd see her after school, and he'd gone. And as soon as he'd gone she thought of all the things she needed to say to him, all the important things, and she should have called him back, but she just sat staring at the phone.

She'd taken the phone up to her room, and when her dad rang off, she'd sat watching Truffle run on his wheel. He was so determined about it – even though he never actually got anywhere with all that running.

"Alice!"

She jumped. "What?"

"I *said*, do you think you could buy me the pencil case for my birthday? Weren't you listening?"

"Sorry," Alice muttered. "I was listening. I just thought of something, that's all."

Lucy eyed her suspiciously and then shrugged. "What's the matter?" she asked. "You've been really weird recently," she added. "For days and days."

"I haven't!" Alice said sharply, but she suspected deep down that Lucy was right, and the weirdness was since she'd found out about Tara and Tilly moving in, the weekend before last. She hadn't been able to stop imagining them at her dad's house, with him all the time.

Now that Tilly lived there, he'd see her more than he saw Alice. That was just wrong.

She wanted to talk to somebody about it, but she couldn't tell her mum. How could Alice talk to her about something that would make her feel so sad? Her mum had been on a couple of dates since her parents had split up, but she'd come home from them, and hugged Alice, and told her she just wasn't ready yet.

There was no way she was going to tell Lucy how wrong everything felt either. Not when Lucy's house was so perfectly *right*. With her mum and dad who never said a cross word to each other, they even thought the same about pencil cases. Lucy wouldn't gloat, exactly, or she wouldn't mean to. But it would be like it was when Lucy first got Smartie. She never stopped talking about her, and every time it made Alice remember that she didn't have a hamster. If she told Lucy, whenever Lucy mentioned her house, Alice would know that secretly Lucy was grateful that she had a proper family. Not like poor Alice.

It was nice having Truffle to talk to – it wasn't as if he could tell her what to do, but he was very sympathetic... Alice was sure he listened. He would race along on his wheel, while she pottered about in her room, but if she came to sit on the window seat, he'd always stop to see what she was doing. He was so tame now, he'd just sit in her hand and wash his whiskers, or nibble a treat, while she told him what was going on. His fur was so soft.

"You *are* being weird, Alice! You're away with the fairies half the day. You're not listening to me properly now! And you wander off when people are talking to you. Ms Hickman told you off twice yesterday, and the second time I don't think you even noticed."

Alice blinked at Lucy. She wasn't sure she even remembered the first time. But knowing that Lucy was right didn't make her feel any better about it. "Well, sorry!" she said crossly. She also knew she was being unfair, and that made her sound even nastier than she felt. "I can't help it if you keep going on and on about boring pencil cases, and your boring mum."

Lucy sucked in a shocked, outraged breath. "She's not boring!"

"She is! Your perfect mum, and your perfect dad, who never argue about anything. Boring!"

Lucy put her head on one side curiously. "You're jealous."

"Of course I'm not, stupid. Who'd want a boring family like yours?"

"You're so mean, Alice MacGregor." Lucy got up, folding her arms and glaring down at

Alice. "You know what? I bet your dad left just to get away from you." She gave a little gulp after she said it, as though she realized what an awful thing it was to say. But she didn't take it back.

Alice blinked away tears, refusing to let Lucy see her cry. She was going to cry though, she couldn't stop herself. Lucy had said the absolute worst thing – the thing that Alice had been trying to stop herself from thinking. The thing that secretly she was afraid was true. Dad had left because he didn't want her any more – and now he'd replaced her with someone else.

"I hate you!" she hissed at Lucy, and she jumped up from the wall, barging past her and dashing away across the playground. She wasn't quite sure where she was going. Just away.

She flung open the door to the corridor – perhaps she'd be able to hide in the toilets, or in the cloakroom, if Ms Hickman wasn't in their classroom. But as she hurled herself through the door, blinded by tears, she thumped straight into someone coming the other way.

"Oi! Watch it!" the boy snapped.

"Leave me alone!"

"I'm trying, *you* barged into *me*!" It was Joe – one of the boys in her class. Alice didn't really know him, he'd only joined the school the year before. He was clever, and he read a lot. And now he'd seen her crying. She couldn't pretend that she wasn't.

"Um, sorry, did you hurt yourself?" He

sounded worried. As though he really did think it was his fault.

"No. Go away. Please! Just leave me alone!" Alice dashed away from him down the corridor towards the girls' loos. Now he'd tell the whole class that she was crying. And Lucy would tell them why.

Everyone would know.

7

The weeks when Alice wasn't going to her dad's house for the weekend, he would usually pick her up from school one evening in the week. The plan was that they would do special things together, like going ice skating, or playing frisbee in the park. But that didn't always happen. Alice had after-school stuff, ballet and art club, and Dad sometimes had work things he had to get done, which meant that they watched TV, or Alice did, while Dad worked on his laptop and pretended he was watching.

That Thursday, after her fight with Lucy,

Alice wished she could go back to Mum's house. She could tell Mum she wasn't feeling well and ask to go to bed. She'd hide under the duvet, warm and breathless, and pretend the day hadn't happened. Mum would bring her hot chocolate, or toast with the crusts cut off, which was only for when Alice was ill.

Or she could get Truffle to play in his maze again – it was put away under her bed. She could tell him how mean Lucy had been. And he'd listen, and she'd know he thought she was right, even though he couldn't say it.

But instead she had to go back with Dad, and Tara and Tilly would be there. It was their house now too – more than it was hers. She was just a visitor.

Tilly went to a school closer to Dad's house,

he explained in the car on the way there, so she and Tara would already be back when they got home.

"Maybe you can watch TV together?" he suggested hopefully.

"I've got homework," Alice muttered. It wasn't actually true; mostly they got homework for the weekends. But Dad wouldn't know that. She hugged her rucksack tightly, pressing it against her front like a shield. She didn't want to do this. Surely Tilly must have a dad as well – why couldn't she go and see him when Alice was coming over? Couldn't they organize it so that she and Tilly never had to meet?

"Tilly's really excited to see you again," Dad went on, determinedly cheerful. "She even drew you a picture!"

Alice rolled her eyes out of the window. Great. Now she was going to have a wannabe little sister trailing around after her all the time she was with Dad.

The picture was on the kitchen table when Alice followed Dad into the house. Tilly was sitting next to it, eating a piece of toast. She didn't say anything when they came in; she just kept eating, and stared at Alice.

Alice glanced at her quickly, and then looked at her feet, out of the window, anywhere but at Tilly.

"Tilly, give Alice your picture!" Tara said brightly. She and Dad were trying so hard.

Tilly pushed the picture across the table. Then she went back to eating her toast.

Alice picked it up. Tilly had drawn a house

that might just about be Dad's house – it had a green door, like the real thing. There was a person in each of the three windows squashed under the roof, and another stick figure standing outside.

"That's you," Tilly said, pressing a buttery finger on to the paper, and stuffing the last corner of toast into her mouth. The felt tip smeared, so that stick-Alice looked a bit like she was melting.

"OK. Um, thank you." Alice swallowed. "Can I go and do my homework upstairs?" she asked Dad.

"You wouldn't like a snack?" Tara asked, a worried frown scrunching up her face. "Toast? Some juice?"

"No, thank you. It's a comprehension, and

it's really hard, and I couldn't do it yesterday because of ballet." It was all a lie, but Alice didn't care. She just wanted to get out.

She hurried up to her room, stepping over the spillage of Barbies and scented pens and hairbands from Tilly's tiny bedroom next door to hers. (Already? She'd only lived there a day; how could she make that much mess?) At least she didn't have to share a room with her, Alice realized suddenly, her stomach twisting at the thought. She arranged some books artistically on her bed and leaned against the wall, twirling a pencil in her fingers. Truffle would be missing her. She always ran up to see him as soon as she got home from school. He would hurry out of his bedroom to see her; he knew that she'd give him something nice, maybe a monkey nut – he got really excited about those, trying to dig the peanuts out of the crinkly shell.

Alice smiled to herself, chewing the end of her pencil. Then she jumped. Tilly was standing in the doorway of her room.

"Um. Yes?" Alice felt like telling her to go away – but that would just get her into trouble with Dad.

"I don't like you," Tilly said. She didn't say it nastily, more as if it was a fact that she thought Alice ought to know.

Alice swallowed. "Oh." What was she supposed to say to that?

"You two girls all right?" Dad bounded up the stairs, and Alice sighed. Too late. She had been curious to see what Tilly said next.

Stupidly, she hadn't even considered that Tilly might hate the thought of her too. Tilly stuck out her tongue and whisked round Dad and away to her own room.

It was so much better, being at Mum's house for the weekend, and not having to worry about Mum forgetting to feed Truffle, or Tilly sleeping in the next-door bedroom. Alice could almost forget how weird school had been on Friday, with no one much to talk to. Lucy hadn't even looked at her all day.

Alice mooched about, feeding Truffle sunflower seeds in between doing bits of her homework and reading the mouse book again, just in case there was anything she'd missed. On Saturday afternoon, she finally got round to making a huge sign out of the side of a cardboard box. It had a string handle so she could hang it on her doorknob whenever she was letting Truffle out.

Maybe she should just leave it up all the time, she wondered, as she hung it out for about the fourth time on Sunday. Truffle was getting so tame now that she felt happy to let him climb all over her while she was doing her homework, or reading. The best thing was, she'd taught him to snuggle up in her pocket. It hadn't really been difficult – she'd just put another dog biscuit in there the first time, and now he thought pockets were full of good things.

Alice had lined her pocket with a pretty embroidered handkerchief that her Gran had given her – which she couldn't see herself using for anything else. The handkerchief was just to make it easier to clean the pocket out afterwards. Truffle was very clean – he had a little tray in one corner of the cage that he used as a toilet – but he might forget, and Alice didn't fancy finding fossilized mouse poo in her pocket next time she wore this hoodie.

She shifted restlessly, and ran a gentle hand over the tiny bulge that was her mouse. "It's all right for you, you've got peanuts in there," she murmured. "I'm starving." Truffle stuck his head out of her pocket at the sound of her voice, but then he ducked back inside. He'd been sleeping, Alice thought. It was such a pity to make him go back in the cage.

Unless she didn't, of course. Alice smiled to herself. She'd have to be careful – Mum would have a fit if she found out, and there was Tiger, of course. . . She'd have to look out for the cat. But why shouldn't she take Truffle downstairs? Just for a moment, while she found some raisins, or an apple, or something. She could share it with Truffle.

She stole out of her room, pulling the door closed behind her, and crept down the stairs. Tiny, feather-light Truffle suddenly felt huge in her pocket, as though anyone would be able to see him straight away. Alice looked around anxiously for Tiger – was this stupid? What if Tiger smelled Truffle and leaped up at her pocket? But she could see out of the landing window that Tiger was prowling down the garden, probably off after the squirrels who came to next door's bird table. Alice breathed out, a little shakily, and tried to look normal as she went on downstairs. It was quite hard to do, as she couldn't think what normal really looked like. Just not guilty...

"Hello, sweetie. What are you up to?" her mum called from the living room.

"Just playing with Truffle upstairs. I had my sign out," Alice added quickly. It was actually true... "Can I have a snack, I'm starving? An apple? Can I have a bit of cheese with it?"

"Course." Her mum was marking again. She didn't even look at Alice properly. Alice felt like yelling, "I've got a mouse in my pocket!" just to make her listen.

She hurried back up to her room. The door was open a little – hadn't she shut it? Alice was almost sure she had, she had been so careful over the last few days with Truffle, and remembering to put the sign out. She sped up, cupping her hand over her pocket to stop Truffle bouncing about.

The first thing she saw when she got into her room was Tiger, sitting by the mouse cage and peering hopefully inside.

"No! Bad cat! Shoo!" Alice pushed him off the window seat, and flapped her hands at him. Tiger strolled smugly across her floor and out, refusing to run. Alice shut the door with a slam as soon as his sausage-fat tail had flicked round the edge, and sighed shakily.

Had she not shut the door properly? Perhaps she had only pulled it to. The cat was big enough to lean his front paws against the door and shove it open. Whatever had happened, Tiger was watching out for Truffle now, it was quite clear. He was clever and determined, even if he was lazy.

Alice peered carefully into her pocket and saw that Truffle was still in there, quite safe. He was curled up asleep, a flap of the handkerchief wrapped over him, as if he was tucked up in a little bed.

Now that Tiger had sniffed him out, how could she leave the tiny mouse behind next weekend?

8

Alice was almost sure that she couldn't leave Truffle for a whole weekend with Mum again. Mum and Tiger. She worried about it all week, especially at school. It was quite a good distraction from being lonely without Lucy. Alice kept forgetting they weren't talking, and turning round to whisper something to her. But then the way Lucy's shoulders were hunched over would remind her, and she'd stare back down at her work.

She couldn't decide whether it was a stupid idea to take Truffle with her to school, and Dad's. Or the only thing she could do?

She kept wavering between the two.

But by Friday she had decided. It was the way Tiger kept turning up outside her door, pacing backwards and forwards and sniffing underneath. And then when he saw her coming up the stairs, he'd get really excited and stand up on his hind legs, pawing at the door, as though he thought she was going to let him in to catch a mousy snack! He didn't learn, either, he kept coming back, even though every time she said "No, Tiger!" and pushed him away. Alice had seen videos of cats opening door handles. She was not leaving Truffle in her room all weekend. She was worried enough about Tiger trying to break in while she was at school.

Truffle had looked so lonely when she

came home after her last weekend at Dad's too. Mum just putting food in the cage and not even stroking him wasn't enough. He needed someone to love him. Alice needed someone to love her too, and she wasn't sure whether she was going to get that at Dad's house. But if she had Truffle in her pocket, she wouldn't care if Tilly didn't like her. She almost wouldn't care if Dad liked Tilly more than he liked her.

On Friday morning, she made up Truffle's little travel box with lots of bedding, and some food in one of the pots her mum used for packed lunches – it was smaller than Truffle's heavy china food bowl. She put another one of the pots in her rucksack so she could give him a drink of water. That was her only worry –

the travel box didn't have a water bottle in it because Truffle wasn't meant to be in there for very long. But she was sure she'd be able to sneak him a drink.

Alice snuggled Truffle in her hands and then slipped him gently inside the box. She wished she could have put his little felt bedroom in too, but she was hoping that when Mum couldn't see him over the weekend, she would just think that he was asleep in there. It would be a bit obvious if his bedroom had disappeared.

The box just about fitted in the bottom of her rucksack – it was lucky that she always had school dinner on Friday, she'd never have got her lunch box in there too.

Alice's mum dropped her off at school on

the way to the secondary school where she worked, which was only a bit further down the road. Alice carefully climbed out of the car, cradling her rucksack, trying to hold the bag with her weekend stuff too.

"Put your rucksack on your back," her mum pointed out, smiling. "You'll never manage, carrying them both like that."

Alice nodded, resting the bags on the pavement. "I will. Bye, Mum. See you on Sunday night. Don't forget to feed Truffle!" She felt guilty saying it, but after all the fuss she'd made last time, Mum would think it was weird if she didn't say anything. She stood waving as Mum drove off, and then looked at the playground. She didn't really want to go in. It was more than a week now and she still hadn't made up with Lucy – she wasn't sure she actually could. They'd both said such horrible things.

There were other people she could talk to, of course. But even though the girls in her class were friendly, they kept asking her why she and Lucy weren't talking any more, and Alice couldn't tell them, not without explaining what Lucy had said about her dad. She wasn't repeating that to anyone – it still felt too much as though it might be true.

Alice wrapped her rucksack against her front with one arm, and dragged the other bag behind her into school. She sat down, leaning against the wall, with her rucksack tucked under her arm. She didn't want anyone kicking a football into Truffle, or tripping over him. She opened the zip of her bag and peered in, lifting the cardigan she'd draped over the top of the box, in case anyone happened to look.

It seemed to take ages for the bell to go as Alice sat there, flinching every time someone ran past. Ms Hickman was on playground duty as well, and she kept looking over. Alice wished she wouldn't. Ever since she'd heard Mum and Dad arguing about Parents' Evening, she'd had a feeling that Ms Hickman was worrying about her, and she hated it. Alice was pretty sure that Ms Hickman knew about her fight with Lucy too. It was obvious they weren't hanging around together any more. So now Alice was the sad child with the problem family and no friends... She set her face in a grimly cheerful smile as Ms Hickman walked past her again.

Alice had never thought that school could be so slow. But now she was thinking about it as a mouse would, a mouse whose heart beat 670 times a minute. Everything must seem ten times slower for Truffle, Alice worried, listening to Lara chattering on about her weekend trip to a castle. He was probably sick of being in the box already. She would have to stay behind at break and let him out. She could put him in the pocket of her school cardigan – it was a jersey one, the same kind of fabric as her hoody. It would feel familiar. She'd even brought the handkerchief to line it with. But then someone might spot him in class, or he could jump out in the playground. He could easily get squashed by a load of boys playing football. It was too dangerous.

By break time, she could hardly keep still, she was so desperate to check on Truffle. The rest of the class seemed to take hours to go out to the playground – Alice nearly snapped at two of the girls who couldn't find their jackets. But then, at last, everyone had gone. Alice slipped into the book corner, where she'd be hidden a little by the bookcases, and gently lifted the travel box out of her rucksack. She opened it up carefully – she couldn't risk Truffle jumping out if he was really sick of being shut up in there. But he'd been asleep, it looked like. He uncurled himself and nuzzled at Alice's fingers while she tidied up the scattered bits of food. Then she dribbled a little water from her bottle into the spare pot and put it in front of Truffle, holding on to it so he couldn't tip it over. She looked at him anxiously – was he going to understand what to do? He'd always drunk from a bottle before. But he rested his front paws on the edge and lapped up a few drops. "I'd leave it there for you," Alice whispered, "but I think you'd spill it. Is that enough?" She took the pot out again and sat cross-legged, making a bowl out of her skirt for Truffle to run about in.

"What have you got in there?" someone asked, and Alice was so shocked that she jumped, and Truffle scurried on to the floor. She had to grab him before he disappeared under the bookcase.

"It isn't anything!" Alice gasped, trying to snuggle Truffle up in her hands. But he didn't want to be hidden. He nudged his nose against her fingers curiously, tickling her with his whiskers. "Where did you come from? No one was here, I checked."

Joe was leaning over the bookcase and staring at Truffle. The last time she'd spoken to him was when she'd almost knocked him over after her fight with Lucy. He'd seen her crying. But actually, Alice thought, he hadn't told anyone – or not as far as she knew, anyway.

Lucy didn't go and tell everyone either, Alice realized suddenly. *She can't have done, or Lara and Maisie would have told* me; *they love stirring up gossip. She kept quiet, and so did I. . .*

Joe ducked his head shyly. "I was behind

the bookcase," he admitted. "I just didn't want to go out. Ms Hickman always tries to get me to play football with the others, and I've got this really good book. I didn't think anyone would notice." He gave her a hopeful look. "I won't tell you've got a mouse if you don't tell about me."

"All right," Alice agreed. "Please don't tell. I only brought him in because I can't leave him at home. I'm going to my dad's this weekend, and my mum won't look after him properly. Not to be mean, she just doesn't like mice. She thinks his tail's creepy."

"He's very tame," Joe said, watching Truffle peering in at the cuff of Alice's cardigan. "Will he go—? Oh, yes, I guess he will then." He laughed and then looked round nervously at the door in case he'd been too loud. "Sorry! It looks so funny, there's this little bump going up your sleeve. . ."

"I should probably put him back in; it isn't long till the end of break." Alice sighed, and gently caught Truffle as he appeared at the neck of her cardigan. "Come on, sweetie pie. I wish I could just put you in my pocket, but someone would spot you, I bet." She slipped him back into the box.

Joe looked at it admiringly. "Like a mini mouse house."

"He isn't really supposed to be in it all day, though." Alice tucked it back into her rucksack, just as the bell went. "Thanks," she whispered to Joe, as the others started to race into the classroom.

*

At lunchtime, Joe appeared next to Alice as she was putting her plate on the trolley to be cleared away. "Are you, um, going back to the classroom?" he asked, waggling his eyebrows.

Alice put her hand over her mouth to stop herself laughing, his face was so funny.

"Yes," she whispered through her fingers.

"Can I come and see him again?" Joe asked, looking hopeful.

"S'pose so. You could keep watch."

"All right! I had an idea, about how you could let him run around for a bit. I'll show you."

They followed the rest of the class heading out towards the playground, but then ducked sideways into the classroom instead. No one else was there, and Alice went straight to check on Truffle – she had hated leaving him, but they had to line up to go to lunch, and Ms Hickman would have noticed if she hadn't gone. Alice hadn't been able to think of a reason to take her rucksack to the dining hall, either.

"He definitely wants to come out," she told Joe. "He's awake and he's sniffing around the edges of the box."

"Bring him over here." Joe beckoned her over to the tables where their project work was all set up. "Look, you can let him run around in my villa!"

Joe had got the world's largest number of house points for his Roman project – he'd made a huge Roman house out of cardboard boxes, all painted, and it even had a mosaic floor cut out of hundreds of tiny little squares.

"Really? You wouldn't mind?" Alice went pink. "I mean, he might poo... I'd clear it up."

"Fine by me. I'm a bit sick of it, anyway. It took me and my dad ages to make, and it got a bit boring, painting it all. I bet my dad won't let me throw it away either, it's going to be in my room for ever. It's more use as a mouse playground."

"I make him little mazes and things in my room," Alice agreed. "This is like a luxury one." She set Truffle down in the middle of the house, and he sniffed curiously at the clay feast that Joe had made. "Oh, not that! Here, look, sunflower seeds." She put a couple into one of the little bowls, and they laughed as Truffle scurried down the table after them, weaving his way past Joe's tiny dishes.

"He's like a monster mouse. We should borrow Alfie's gladiator scene too, he could be the wild beasts."

The classroom door banged, and Alice jumped round, certain they'd been caught. But it wasn't Ms Hickman glaring at them – instead Lucy was standing in the doorway.

"Oh. . ." Lucy looked at them uncomfortably. "I just came to get my coat."

Joe and Alice stared at her in silence as she hurried into the cloakroom. They could hear her rustling around, and then she came back with her pink fleecy jacket on. Her cheeks were pink too, and she looked miserable. She didn't even glance at Joe and Alice as she went past.

"Lucy!" She was almost at the door.

"What?"

"Um. . ." Alice didn't know – she'd just hated seeing her friend dashing past, too hurt or cross even to say hello. Alice wasn't sure which.

"Her mouse is in my Roman villa," Joe put in, trying to help.

Lucy's mouth dropped open. "You mean it?"

"Look!" Alice stepped back to let Lucy see.

"Why's he in school?" Lucy whispered. "Oh, he's cute!"

"You know that my mum really doesn't like mice," Alice said. "Well, I've got to go to my dad's for the weekend again and she didn't feed him properly last time. And he missed me. And Tiger wants to eat him. So I brought him with me."

"Oh." Lucy looked at her sideways. "I didn't mean it, about your dad."

"Me neither – about your mum, and the pencil case. I'm really sorry. I wish my parents agreed about everything like yours."

Alice swallowed. "My dad's got a new girlfriend, and she's got a little girl. She's called Tilly. Tilly can't stand me. And I think my dad likes her better than me."

"I bet he doesn't." Lucy folded her arms. "But he's got to be nice to her, hasn't he? My parents are way meaner to me than they are to anybody else. When my cousin broke a plate, my mum just smiled and said it didn't matter. She'd make me pay out of my pocket money if I did that. And afterwards she said my cousin was a little horror."

"That's true." Joe nodded. "My dad's the same. He says it's like, company manners. Not taking the biggest cake even when it's your party, and that sort of stuff."

"What exactly are you three doing indoors

when you're supposed to be out in the playground?"

"Put him in your pocket!" Joe breathed.

Alice felt Joe and Lucy step in front of her as Ms Hickman walked across the classroom. She scooped Truffle out of the villa and slipped him into her pocket.

"Sorry, Ms Hickman – they're helping me," Joe explained. "I've lost my book. It's from the library, I was really worried and Alice and Lucy said they'd help me look for it. My dad'll be really cross if I've lost it. It's about Romans," he added.

Ms Hickman smiled, glancing over at the villa. "You're still reading about them? That's wonderful. But you know you shouldn't be inside. Two more minutes to look, that's all!"

"Did you do that on purpose?" Alice whispered to Joe, as they scurried round, looking under the tables and lifting up piles of coats. "Make her remember all your house points?"

"Yes. She keeps showing off the villa anytime people visit," Joe muttered back. "And I really have lost the book somewhere. It worked though, didn't it? She didn't even tell us off, hardly. Is he in your pocket?"

"Mmm. But I can't put him back in the box, not with her here."

"Will he stay in there?" Lucy asked. "Oh, look, I've found the book!" she said loudly, pulling it out from under a pile of homework books, and holding it out to Joe.

"You've found it?" Ms Hickman called, from

over by her desk. "Well done. You may as well stay in now – it's only a couple of minutes till the end of lunch."

"If he tries to come out of your pocket I'll warn you," Lucy said, eyeing Alice's cardigan.

"Me too." Joe snatched the tiny bowl from his villa, still full of sunflower seeds. "Stick that in with him."

"He'll probably eat the cardboard!" Alice whispered.

"Good – he'll like that, won't he?"

Lucy sighed. "I wish I'd brought Smartie to school, but she's too fat to fit in my pocket." She sank her hands into her coat pockets, as if she wished they were full of plump hamsters. "Oh, but I've got raisins in here, look. He can have those too, they're Smartie's favourite." She handed Alice the box. "I can see his whiskers," she whispered. "He's so cute. I'm really sorry. Can I sit next to you again? Properly, not squashed down the other end of the table?"

Alice nodded. "Yes. Please! We have to not let Lara and Maisie see Truffle." She cupped her hand round her cardigan pocket – she could feel Truffle wriggling, as he started to nibble away the corner of the raisin box. It had to be a mouse dream come true, a whole box of sweetness. "Thanks," she whispered to Lucy and Joe as the bell rang.

9

"Why doesn't she go to bed when I do?"
Tilly stood in the living-room doorway in her
pyjamas, kicking at the door frame with her
furry boots.

Alice looked round in surprise. She was
watching TV with Dad – and Tara, but
actually, Tara had voted with Alice on what
to watch, so it didn't matter so much that she
was there too.

This was the first night that she and Tilly
had both slept at Dad's house. Dad and Tara's
house, she had to say now, she supposed. The
issue of bedtime hadn't come up before.

"I'm older than you," she said, trying not to sound as though she thought it was obvious (even though it was).

"You're not bigger than me!" Tilly flashed back.

Alice laughed. She was so much bigger than Tilly that it was funny, but Tilly screeched and flew across the room, grabbing at Alice's dressing gown. "You're not! You're not!"

"Get off me!" Alice shoved her back – not even hard – but Tara was already trying to grab Tilly, and Tilly's elbow somehow bumped Tara's shoulder, and suddenly everything was quiet and Tara was rubbing her arm.

Tilly stared at Tara, her eyes huge and round – and then she turned on Alice, screaming, "You hurt my mum!"

"I didn't!" Alice said shakily. "It was you."

"It was an accident." Tara rubbed her eyes and tried to smile at Alice. "Tilly, Alice is older than you. She goes to bed later. That's what big sisters do."

"She – isn't – my – sister!"

"I don't want you for a sister either!" Alice snapped, getting up and stomping out. "I'm going to my room anyway. But I'm not going to bed!" she yelled at the five-year-old from the safety of the stairs. "Because I'm bigger than you and I don't have to!"

She thought Dad might make her come back, but he didn't. It was good, Alice told herself as she marched furiously upstairs. Now she could be in her room to make sure Truffle was OK, without Dad wondering why.

But what if it was like this every time she came? She could only see Dad with Tilly there too, spoiling everything? It made her stomach feel cold.

"She's horrible," she whispered to Truffle, sitting under her duvet, with his box open on her lap. His little chocolate face peered out at her, his whiskers shaking. Then he climbed out of the box and up the sleeve of her pyjamas. His tiny pinprick claws tickled as he scrabbled his way up, all the way to her shoulder. He sat there, just nibbling the sunflower seeds she handed him, while Alice stared into the darkness of her room.

"You need to go to bed now, Alice." Dad's voice. She hadn't even heard him come upstairs. How long had she been sitting there with Truffle? Alice froze, silently begging Dad not to look under her duvet.

"Night then," she muttered, turning away from him to make it clear she didn't want a goodnight hug.

"Don't forget to do your teeth. And, Alice?"

"Yes?"

"We'll do something nice tomorrow, all right? It'll be all of us, but we'll find something special for just you and me."

"OK."

"Night, Alice."

Alice lay curled up under her duvet, with Truffle in the pocket on the front of her onesie. She wasn't sleepy yet, so she was reading with her little torch. Or trying to. It was hard to concentrate. She kept thinking about Tilly, and Dad, and Tara. And what Mum would think of it all.

She was planning to put Truffle back into his box before she tried to go to sleep – even though he was so tame, she didn't think he'd stay with her all night, especially if he ran out of food. If he disappeared off into the house, it would be hard to get him back again, and she didn't want Tara or Tilly being the ones to find him. She wasn't even sure what Dad thought about mice. She'd told him about Truffle, of course, but all he'd said was that having a pet sounded fun. He hadn't been enthusiastic, exactly.

Truffle was quite still, curled up in her warm pocket, and Alice was wondering if she could put him back in the box without waking him up, when she first heard the noise. It took her a few heart-stopping seconds to realize that someone was crying. Alice had never had a brother or sister so she wasn't used to hearing a younger child crying in the night. It was a soft, quiet noise, hardly there but still horribly eerie. And impossible to ignore.

Alice sat up in bed, waiting for Tara or Dad to come up the stairs to comfort Tilly. But they didn't – perhaps they couldn't hear? They had the television on. Alice sighed huffily and lay down. She wasn't going to go and tell them. Tilly could manage by herself.

Except that the noise didn't stop. Little breathy sobs and choking catches in her throat. Every so often there'd be a moment of quiet, and Alice would think that Tilly had cried herself to sleep – but then it was just a breath and she'd start again.

"Be quiet!" Alice muttered at the wall. That was why she could hear, of course. Tilly's bed and hers were next to each other, with just a thin wall in between. If they ever decided to talk to each other, they could probably tap out secret messages. It could even be fun.

Tilly didn't stop.

Alice got out of bed and stalked furiously next door. "Will you stop it?" she hissed at the doorway. "I can't sleep."

"I can't either," Tilly gasped out.

"Just stop crying!"

"I can't!" She wavered it out, like the end of a song.

Tilly's face was white in the darkness, and

she looked very small curled up in the corner of the bed. She had a teddy, all squashed up in her arms as if she couldn't let him go.

"What are you crying for anyway?" Alice asked crossly. She was cross with herself as much as with Tilly – cross because she didn't hate her any more.

Tilly gulped and bubbled. "I don't like it here."

"Oh. Me neither."

"I want to go back to our flat. This house is horrible. And you are."

"You were horrible to me first," Alice pointed out.

Tilly was silent for a moment. She'd almost stopped crying and she seemed to be thinking about what Alice had said.

"You aren't having my mum."

"I've got a mum!"

Alice wanted to say, *You're the one taking my dad*. But she couldn't, even though it felt like it was true. Dad had told her in the car that Tilly's dad hadn't been around since she was tiny. If she'd been angry still, she'd have said it. But Tilly being so little and pale in the dark bedroom had just made her feel sad instead.

She sighed. "Do you want to see a secret? You'll have to come in my room, my torch is in there."

"Mum said I'm not allowed in your room."

"It's my room, you can if I say so."

Tilly didn't say anything, but she tucked the bear under her arm and wriggled out of her duvet, following Alice next door like a little ghost.

"Look." Alice turned on the torch and propped it on her bedside table so that it shone like a spotlight. Then she slipped her hand in her pocket to pull out Truffle.

Except he wasn't there.

"What is it?" Tilly peered down at Alice's hands.

"Nothing, it's nothing, I've lost him!"

"Who? Your bear?"

Alice smiled without meaning to. Tilly's words had make her think of a real bear. "No, a mouse, how could I have a bear in my pocket? It's my pet mouse. He's chocolate-coloured. He must have climbed out of my pocket when I came into your room."

"There's a mouse in my bedroom? A real mouse?"

Alice looked worriedly at Tilly, and nodded. Was she going to scream? But the little girl's tear-stained face had changed. Her eyes were shining excitedly in the yellowish torchlight.

"Can he go in my dolls' house?" she begged.

"He can if we find him," Alice said, picking up the pot of food and then taking Tilly's hand and hurrying her back to her own little room. If they found him she'd let Tilly hold him, even, she decided. She'd do anything. She scanned the torch over the landing – no little brown mouse. How could she not have noticed Truffle climbing out of her pocket? It must have been when she was fussing about Tilly.

"We should put the light on," she said anxiously, reaching for the switch.

"Mum will see." Tilly shook her head. "It shines down the stairs. Even if I shut the door, she can tell!"

Alice sucked in a worried breath. "All right. Just stand still then. Listen. We might hear him if he's moving around."

But there was nothing, not even a scrabble. Alice felt like crying. She was so stupid. She should just have left Truffle at home, he would have been fine. Now she'd lost him.

"What do we do?" Tilly whispered.

"We have to tempt him back." Alice tried not to sniff. "I'll put some food down for him."

"In the dolls' house?" Tilly asked hopefully.

She pulled Alice's arm so that the torch lit up the pink and white house standing in the corner of the room. It had a front that folded open, swinging out on hinges so you could play with the rooms inside. It was beautiful. If Alice hadn't been so worried, she would have been jealous.

"I suppose. . ."

Tilly crouched down, pushing open the front door and wedging it with what looked like a tiny loo. A lot of the furniture seemed to be sitting on the stairs.

Alice laid a little trail of mouse food up the front steps and pulled the handkerchief out of her onesie for Truffle to lie on.

"He wouldn't like to sleep in the bedroom?" Tilly asked, looking a bit disappointed.

"I don't think he understands about beds," Alice explained. She sat down, wrapping her arms round her knees. "Now we just have to wait for him." *And hope he really is in here somewhere,* she added to herself.

She swallowed back a miserable sort of laugh. Truffle was going to be very bored with his plain cage, after a Roman mansion at lunchtime and a smart pink cottage now.

Tilly looked impatiently at the house, as though she expected a mouse to march up the front steps straight away. But then she went over to her bed and fetched her duvet, wrapping it around her shoulders. Then she looked at Alice, and frowned, and laid a corner of it over her bare feet.

*

The noise that woke Alice was tiny. Just a little pattering noise – one that she knew. The noise of a sunflower seed shell being nibbled away and dropped. He was back.

"Tilly, look," she breathed, reaching out to shake the younger girl's shoulder. "Keep still, all right? He doesn't know you yet."

Tilly woke up, blinking. She was curled on the floor, half on top of Alice's legs now, which was nice, because it was chilly, even though it wasn't the middle of the night. There was light coming through Tilly's curtains; the room was greyish-dim, but it was definitely morning. They'd slept all night on the floor.

Truffle was sitting on the front steps of the dolls' house, nibbling at the food they'd left out. He looked quite smug, as though he'd enjoyed his night-time adventuring. Maybe he liked exploring here, Alice thought. He could probably smell there wasn't a cat around.

Tilly held her breath, staring at the doll-sized mouse in her house.

"He *is* chocolate-coloured," she whispered to Alice.

"That's why he's called Truffle." Alice reached out gently and picked up a peanut from the floor, holding it out to Truffle in her hand. He climbed on to her fingers at once and sat there eating the nut, gazing at Alice and Tilly.

"Can I stroke him?" Tilly looked entranced.

"If you're gentle." Alice held her cupped hands out to Tilly, and the little girl ran one

careful finger down the mouse's cocoa fur.

"Will you always bring him, when you stay?"

"I don't know. I'm not supposed to have him here at all. We could ask, I suppose."

Someone took a breath, behind her, and she looked round to see her dad standing in the doorway. He looked confused, and a bit worried that there was suddenly a mouse, but pleased at the same time. Tara was behind him, looking at Tilly.

Alice looked at her too, her dark hair all tangled, and her eyes shining as Truffle sniffed her fingers. She nodded thoughtfully. Somehow it didn't feel as though she was in the wrong place, not any more.

HOLLY has always loved animals.
As a child she had two dogs, a
cat, and at one point, nine gerbils
(an accident). Holly's other love is
books. Holly now lives in Reading
with her husband, three sons
and three very spoilt cats.